Lord Banjo
the Royal Pooch

Lord Banjo
the Royal Pooch

Banjo Penn
& Kathy Manos Penn
Illustrated by Raw Spoon

MOUNTAIN ARBOR PRESS

MOUNTAIN ARBOR
PRESS
Alpharetta, GA

This is a work of fiction. Names, characters, businesses, places, and events are either the products of the author's imagination or are used in a fictitious manner. Any resemblance to actual persons, living or dead, or actual events is purely coincidental.

Copyright © 2017 by Kathy Manos Penn

All rights reserved. No part of this book may be reproduced or transmitted in any form or by any means, electronic or mechanical, including photocopying, recording, or any information storage and retrieval system, without permission in writing from the author.

ISBN: 978-1-63183-140-9

Library of Congress Control Number: 2017910261

10 9 8 7 6 5 4 3 2   0 7 1 2 1 7

Printed in the United States of America

⊛This paper meets the requirements of ANSI/NISO Z39.48-1992 (Permanence of Paper)

Cover art and illustrations by Raw Spoon at rawspoon.com

To Jon Voorhees,

who first suggested that Lord Banjo write a book.

Dogs do speak, but only to those who know how to listen.

—Orhan Pamuk, novelist

Table of Contents

Acknowledgments	xi
Chapter 1: My Royal Life	1
Chapter 2: The Royal Family	19
Chapter 3: Summer Sojourns	31
Chapter 4: A Royal Holiday Season	79

Acknowledgments

A special thank-you to Beverly Herbert, a.k.a. Miss Beverly, who inspired Lord Banjo to write summer camp e-mails, and to Linda Jordan Genovese, who edited early drafts.

Chapter 1

My Royal Life

Long ago and far away, a puppy was born. He was taken from his doggie mom and sent to live with a family who had dogs and cats and birds and rabbits and many, many children. With so many mouths to feed, it wasn't long before the family put the puppy up for adoption. He could not believe his good fortune when he arrived at his next home. There he settled in with his forever family and discovered the best was yet to come.

I've always known I was exceptional in many ways—my thick, black, wavy coat, my white chest, my white paws, my big brown eyes—but it turns out I'm even more special than I thought. Don't act so shocked; I have proof of how remarkable I am. As a gift for my dad, I had my DNA analyzed. Mum, Dad, and I were all pleasantly surprised—dare I say impressed—by my lineage.

One branch of my family tree is all golden retriever. Even though my adoption papers labeled me a flat-coated retriever mix (maybe because of my beautiful black coloring), I've always *acted* like an easygoing golden.

Given the bloodline on the other side of my tree, I'm calling the goldens the *common* side. Why? Because on this branch, one great-grandparent is a Great Pyrenees. Cool! Did you know that the breed dates back to 1800 BC? Even better, did you know that Louis XIV, the Sun King, declared the Great Pyrenees to be the Royal Dogs of France? That's why, from this day forth, I shall be known as Lord Banjo—not Banjo Boy, Little Boy, or the little boy in the fuzzy suit, as my dad calls me. How unbecoming!

Granted, one of my great-grandparents was a combo golden retriever and Australian shepherd, but I'm giving more weight to my Great Pyrenees great-grandparent. After all, those dogs *do weigh* the most. Those majestic white animals may weigh as much as 160 pounds, so I'm on the trim side at only 80 pounds. Mum and Dad should stop thinking I weigh a tad much, as I come by my regal bearing and imposing size honestly.

And, for goodness' sake, I see no need to spend time on the working-class origins of my one Australian shepherd/golden retriever great-grandparent. Clearly, my royal blood has much more bearing. It matters not that the DNA analysis labels me a golden retriever, Great Pyrenees, Australian shepherd cross in that order; I'm exercising my royal prerogative to rearrange the order and claim the Great Pyrenees as my number-one ancestor. I get my calm and friendly demeanor from both the goldens and Great Pyrenees, but have none of the energetic traits of that rowdy Australian shepherd. That's right, Mum and Dad should start describing me as calm—not lazy.

Now that you know my ancestry, please let it be known far and wide that I am due royal treatment from one and all. I hereby decree that I shall:

- Cease hearing complaints about the *royal* black hair I leave all over the house.
- Be welcomed in my parents' bed, especially since I so graciously let the cat sleep on *all* of my dog beds.
- Suffer no recriminations when I help myself to the cat food that Puddin' leaves in her dish.

- Be served plenty of people food and tasty gourmet dog food.
- Be regularly thanked by my parents for gracing them with my royal presence.

Hear ye, hear ye, life shall henceforth be splendid for Lord Banjo.

When you're a Royal Dog, you have quite a few people looking after you—not just the Royal Mum and Dad. I have a Royal Groomer and several Royal Critter Sitters. Little did I know, Miss Beverly, one of my favorite critter sitters, was about to become known as the Royal Physician. It's possible she may end up with a much less pleasant title depending on how long she has me on this new starvation diet. That's right, at her direction, the Royal Mum and Dad are starving me.

Ever since I spent two nights at her house, she has apparently been biting her tongue about my royal figure. No matter that our *real* veterinarian has never suggested I'm too big. Mum has asked, but the answer has always been, "No, Lord Banjo's eighty pounds are just fine."

They were fine, that is until Miss Beverly joined the Royal Parents and me on a trip. As is my due, she spent lots of time on the floor snuggling with me and whispering in my ear. I like her so much; I even slept in her bedroom the first night instead of with Mum and Dad.

My entourage escorted me to breakfast the next morning. You know we Royal Dogs must promenade so our subjects can see and admire us. I was reclining beneath the outdoor breakfast table when Dad asked for a doggie bag. That's when Miss Beverly lost it. She was horrified at all the doggie bags my parents had been bringing me and let go with a diatribe about my diet. She declared I was too heavy and that my weight would soon cause me joint problems. With that, she laid out a diet plan for me.

My mind was swirling with indignation: *Give up doggie bags? Who put her in charge? Has she lost her mind?*

"*Excusez-moi*," I barked. "Don't I get any say in this plan? What if I go on more walks, maybe strap weights around my ankles, or start doing jumping jacks? Anything but a diet!" Somehow, no one felt it necessary to respond to my plaintive pleas. The result? Mum and Dad are starving me.

Before this distressing turn of events, we had a lovely routine established. Just picture this:

- Mum lets me out in the morning, and I come back in and finish whatever milk remains in the cat's dish.

- Dad gives me my yummy joint supplement and a chunk of bacon as he prepares breakfast and then lets me lick the plate.

- I lick Mum's plate too, and throughout the day, I finish up the dabs of food the finicky cat leaves in her dish. Yes, Puddin', I'm talking about you.

- For lunch, I get chunks of ham from Dad and get to lick Mum's salad bowl. A boy's got to have his greens, you know.

- At dinner, I finally get my big bowl of dry food, with scraps from the dinner plates. Boy, how I love the nights we have salmon or pork chops.

Do you see anything wrong with this diet? I certainly don't. *Mais non*, the Royal Physician has put a stop to all of that. I'm on new dry food, and I'm getting a significantly reduced amount of that plus a *huge* reduction in scraps. I get to lick plates, but only if they're empty already, no chunks of anything. And whenever I look at Dad with longing in my eyes, he says, "Talk to Dr. Beverly."

Not only am I starving, I'm concerned I'll lose my royal figure if this keeps up. What would my great-grandparents think if I were to waste away to nothing? Would they think me unfit to carry on the Great Pyrenees lineage as the Royal Dogs of the French court? Worse yet, might others mistake me for a commoner? I'm tempted to point my royal paw at Dr. Beverly and bark, "Off with her head," but I'm a kind and gentle ruler and will refrain . . . for now.

Here in the Royal City, we just endured a winter heat wave. We broke a record when temps hit seventy-eight degrees. For some reason, the humans were happy about the weather and could be found frolicking in shorts and tank tops. Since I can't unzip my fuzzy suit, warm weather is not my thing.

A brief rise into the high seventies may not seem all that hot, and at least it wasn't humid, but consider this weather headline: "Warm Winter Bad News for Allergy Sufferers." Why? Because the pollen count has reached the danger zone. Lord Banjo is allergic to quite a few things, and one of them is pollen.

The Royal Mum knew right away the pollen count was high, because she saw me rubbing my nose on my dog beds. I get itchy all over, not just on my nose, but all the way up and down my body. Unless I start my daily dose of allergy meds, I'll soon be rubbing my royal body all along the side of Mum and Dad's bed, and chewing and scratching. I *hate* those little pink pills, but I guess it beats the hot spots I get without them.

I wonder whether my royal ancestors suffered the indignity of having pills shoved down their throats. I liked it much better when Mum packed my pills in peanut butter—that is, until she discovered I'm allergic to that too.

Because it was cooler today, I briefly enjoyed lying in the sun while Mum and Dad worked in the yard, but I was ready to go back in long before they were. Dad made some uncomplimentary remarks about my manhood when I barked to go inside, but he doesn't get it. I know my limits, and my shiny black coat was fast becoming dusty, a sure sign the *itchies* would follow. And *itchies* can lead to the dreaded hot spots.

Perhaps this Royal Dog can banish pollen? If not, I think I'll decree that all pills be buried in hamburgers, or perhaps *foie gras*. Pills tucked in *foie gras*—now that's a grand combination.

Daylight saving time is here, but I try not to let that change affect my morning routine. That means I want the Royal Mum to get up, let me outside, and start the coffee at 6:30 a.m.-ish, no matter what the clock says. I can be a bit flexible by letting her sleep in maybe thirty minutes, but a whole hour is asking too much.

This morning when she ignored my nudging her hand, I gave a few short barks spaced a few minutes apart. She tried to ignore those too, but finally escorted me downstairs. When she opened the kitchen door, she was startled by a herd of deer darting away from the driveway into the neighbor's meadow. Me? I wasn't startled; their presence was why I needed to be up and about. Just like me, the deer have their own personal clocks.

I always know they're out there and am especially alert when the bedroom window is open. I wonder why I'm the only one who can hear them. I don't chase them off. Lord Banjo is above that kind of aggressive behavior. I just occasionally remind them that the Royal Nature Preserve is my domain and that it is by my decree they're permitted to enjoy it. They freely roam our yard, until one of us—me, or the Royal Mum or Dad—appears outside. Then they retreat beyond the tree line, where they seem quite content to graze in the meadow, or perhaps they're content because the meadow is also just beyond my underground electric fence.

Sometimes, I stand on the porch and watch them watch me, but this morning, I made my way down the driveway and circled the wooded backyard, enjoying the enticing deer aroma while they all gazed at me adoringly. Yes, I am adored, not just because I'm royal, but because the tale of "Banjo and Bambi" has been passed down through the years.

It's an enchanting story. I had only been in residence a month when I came nose to nose with a tiny, wobbly fawn one June morning. I wasn't aggressive in my early days either; I just wanted to touch noses and get a sniff. Bambi stood frozen in place as I stretched my nose to greet him. That encounter didn't last long, as the Royal Mum caught sight of the two of us and rushed to take me in the house. She didn't know me well enough to realize I wouldn't hurt the little thing. Now she understands I'm a benevolent ruler, as do all of Bambi's descendants.

What a glorious day that was. And so it goes. The life of Lord Banjo is splendid indeed.

Lord Banjo the Royal Pooch

Who's a ninja dog? Certainly not I! While I prefer to be called Lord Banjo, as is only my due, I will *answer* to milord, the prince, and even just Banjo, but I draw the line at ninja dog. What on earth is a ninja dog, anyway? I've seen those ugly ninja turtles on TV, and I don't look at all like them. All I know is that, as usual, my dad came up with this latest insulting nickname.

Though some may disagree—that means you, Dad—I'm highly intelligent. In fact, extreme intelligence is one of the defining characteristics of the Great Pyrenees breed. That's why during the warmer months I know to spend my time on the cool tile floor in the Royal Bathroom. Dad may see it as a guest bath, but I know better. I would take over the master bath, but Dad seems to think that's his domain and regularly runs me out of there. I try to sneak in, only to hear, "Banjo, out, out, get out right now!"

I bark back, "Hey, we Great Pyrenees live to protect everyone and everything! How can I be a proper watchdog when Mum's in the shower if I have to lie in the bathroom doorway?"

If I could recline in the master bath at night, I could be doubly sure no predators sneak in to harm the Royal Parents, but Dad is having none of that.

That leaves the hallway bathroom upstairs as mine. I prefer to be wherever Mum is so I can perform my watchdog duties, and the Royal Bathroom is right across from Mum's office and down from the Royal Bedroom. Plus, I can easily shift from my commanding post at the top of the stairs over to the much cooler bathroom—the one sleeping spot in the house that Puddin' hasn't usurped. In the winter, she alternates between sleeping with Mum and Dad in their bed and taking over my bed. She abandons the Royal Parents in the summer, but she can still be found most nights stretched out in the middle of my big, round Royal Bed.

By stretched out, I mean she lies on her back with her little white belly showing and her four white paws in the air. She looks cute that way, but I think she should try lying with her little white belly stretched out on the tile floor so she can be cool like me.

Though Puddin' hangs out in the Royal Bedroom, she is certainly not a watch cat. She may *watch* birds and squirrels, and she may even chirp at them, but only because she wants so badly to be outside chasing them. She's not protecting anyone, and when she goes to sleep, she's dead to the world for hours on end. Anybody could get by her.

That leaves me to perform watchdog duty by regularly patrolling the Royal Bedroom throughout the night to check on Mum and Dad. You can also count on my being there in time to wake Mum up no later than seven and preferably by six. It's most always Mum I wake up, as Dad hasn't been an early riser since he retired oh-so-many years ago. Times were he was up every morning at 5:30 a.m., or so he claims. That, however, was way before my time.

Most of the predawn hours I spend holding down the bathroom floor. You may recall that my Great Pyrenees heritage gives me a rather imposing frame, and I'm still coming in at just under eighty pounds despite the starvation diet I'm on. Thus, when I gracefully slide into the royal reclining position, you will occasionally hear a gentle *thud*, as Mum describes it. To me, the royal *thud* indicates all is well, that Lord Banjo is resting, not that I've crashed or am shaking the house or any other derogatory description the Royal Parents come up with.

That sound woke my dad the other night, and he got up to see whether we had an intruder. Silly man, the house alarm didn't go off, but I guess he was groggy and not thinking clearly. Despite his foggy brain, he *did* notice I wasn't lying by Mum's bedside, and so he checked the Royal Bathroom before heading downstairs.

Sure enough, I was lying on the cool bathroom floor with my nose peeking out the doorway. It's nice that he checked on me, as I've gotten stuck in there on occasion. No laughing allowed! Sometimes I'm so relaxed I roll over in my sleep and accidentally push the door shut. I bamboozled the critter sitter one evening when she couldn't find me. She knew she'd left me in the house that morning and I *had* to be inside somewhere. Imagine her surprise—and my relief—when she opened the bathroom door.

Dad has tried to explain away calling me a ninja dog by describing ninjas to me. "Banjo, ninjas dress in black head to toe, even with black masks, and they're respected. Real ninjas can be guardians like you. Those turtles are just cartoons."

I still wasn't satisfied, and barked, "Keep trying, Dad!"

"Well, you *do* look like a ninja, because you're covered in black fur and difficult to see in a dark bathroom, plus ninjas are trim and athletic."

Trim? Athletic? Did I hear him right? That explanation could almost be construed as a compliment. I'm not sure I'm buying it, but all will be forgiven if the term "ninja dog" is *never* uttered again. And, a bit of groveling on Dad's part wouldn't hurt either.

Chapter 2

The Royal Family

Allow me to introduce the members of the best-ever family: the Royal Mum and Dad, Puddin', and Tinker. Puddin' and Tinker can also write, perhaps not as eloquently as I, but if I'm any judge, I believe you'll find them entertaining too!

The Royal Mum and Dad

I was born in New Orleans and don't recall my doggie parents, but I know that one of them passed their Great Pyrenees genes on to me. Since Louis XIV named the Great Pyrenees the Royal Dogs of France, it seems only fitting that I hail from New Orleans, a city founded by the French.

I have my canine parents to thank for my royal roots, but I'm thankful every day for my people parents. So when I say I have the best-ever parents, I mean my two-legged Royal Mum and Dad. Dad calls me a mama's boy, and perhaps that's accurate. After all, it was Mum who found me on Craigslist and changed my name from Nitro to Banjo. Thank goodness! The idea of being called Lord Nitro gives me the willies. She also enrolled me in doggie school so I could learn to be as well behaved as Dad's wonder dog, Tinker.

When I first joined the family, it was clear that Tinker was well established as Dad's favorite, so for the first few years, I mostly hung out with Mum. She worked at home, and we dogs were part of her morning routine. When she grabbed her robe, Tinker and I knew it was time to go downstairs. Mum let us out while she got her first cup of coffee.

Then we accompanied Mum back upstairs to her office, where we knew we'd get our first treats of the day. I took my treats and lay down beneath Mum's desk, but Tinker wanted a treat anytime Mum moved. When Mum got a second cup of coffee, Tinker expected a treat. When Mum walked into the bedroom or fixed breakfast, Tinker wanted a treat. Me? I just snoozed beneath the desk, sometimes so soundly, I snored. Mum says I make a fabulous footrest.

Once Dad was up and about, Tinker stuck to his side. Dad played ball with her and laughed as she wrestled with sticks and dug up rocks. In fact, Dad tended to diss me because I didn't have any interest in balls or sticks or rocks. I've always been content to lie around and have my belly rubbed. Tinker and I looked alike with wavy, black coats, white chests, and white paws, but we were polar opposites in our personalities.

Back in the day, Dad occasionally walked Tinker and me together, though our competition to see who would be in the lead could make for some tense moments. Tinker was a sweet girl, but she was accustomed to being top dog and was awfully competitive.

When Tinker went to Doggie Heaven, we all missed her, but Dad took it especially hard. Soon, even though I didn't chase balls, Dad began to spend more time with me. He discovered I was pretty lovable and that, in addition to being a fantastic footrest, I was a wonderful walker. It wasn't long before we two formed a bond and developed a new morning routine. I may still go downstairs first thing with Mum and start my day beneath her desk, but the action starts when Dad gets up.

Dad gives me my morning meds, feeds me, and then takes me for a walk. The signals that a walk is imminent are the sunglasses coming out of the cabinet, the ball cap going on his head, and the leash coming off the hook. It tickles him that I pay attention and perk up, and then we're off. Some days, I even get a second walk in the afternoon.

Dad's awesome at lots of things, but he has one amazing talent that tops the rest: at six feet two inches tall, he can recline in his easy chair and hang his arm down to rub my royal belly as I lie beside him. That touch is all I require to be a happy boy. When he gets distracted and falls down on the job, I signal him with my royal paw, and the touch resumes.

I may have missed out on growing up with a doggie dad and mom, but I'm sure I have the best-ever two-legged parents.

The Royal Cat, as Told by Puddin'

I agree we have marvelous parents, but I've about had it with this "royal dog" stuff. Why Mum ever started letting the boy dictate stories for her to type is beyond me. Unlike the dog, I am perfectly capable of typing my own stories. After all, as a clever cat, I've spent plenty of time on Mum's keyboard, though until now, I've kept my typing talents hidden. My other office skills—snoozing in file drawers and straightening the desktop—are well known to Mum, and that's why she calls me Puddin' the Office Assistant.

Now, about that dog. Yes, he *was* here before me, and yes, he's certainly larger than I, but he knows full well he's *not* in charge. The silly boy thinks that because his DNA analysis indicates his ancestors are Great Pyrenees, that he is somehow special. Pfftt.

Haven't we all heard of folks who are royal but not all that intelligent or talented? That's Banjo. He's nice enough, easy to get along with, and generous with his many dog beds, but bright or talented? Hardly. His main activities are lying around, taking walks, and eating my cat food when I take a delicate digestive pause between bites. Pretty useless, I'd say.

I, on the other hand, don't require a DNA test to prove how special I am. First, I'm a calico cat with distinctive markings and—as are 99.9 percent of calicos—*female*. Need I say more? I'm also exceptional because I'm a calico-tortoiseshell combo. Talk about a beauty.

We calicos are considered good luck. Good looking and lucky, what a winning combination. We're known for our distinctive orange patches on a white background, and we originated in Egypt. Those ancient Egyptians were awfully smart, and I'm sure that's why you find so many cats in their artwork, not only black cats but calicos too.

Early on, sailors saw us as especially good luck, and Japanese fishermen even kept us on their boats to protect them in storms. You've seen the Fortune Cat figurines in Asian restaurants, right? They originated in Japan as lucky charms, but did you know that the calico version is considered the luckiest?

Enough said about my heritage. If Banjo expects to be called Lord Banjo, then I certainly should be called Princess Puddin'. With or without royal blood, I rightly rule the roost without lifting a paw.

I get first dibs on all the dog beds, sleep with Mum and Dad, and have special blankets on both couches. When I enter the kitchen meowing, someone promptly feeds me. They usually remember that milk is the first course in the morning, but occasionally they mess up, and I turn up my nose until my bowl is correctly filled. Banjo shares his water bowl with me and even his food dish when I'm so inclined.

When I speak in the evenings, Dad knows it's playtime and obliges with the bird and the snake, my favorite toys. He exclaims over my leaps and flips and adores my flying white paws. I take turns in Mum and Dad's laps, but as Dad points out, he has the best belly for kitties. It seems the birds are the only creatures impervious to my demands. No matter how loudly I squeak at them from my window perch, they don't respond. Maybe someday.

And I'm not only acrobatic, I'm smart too. When Mum heads to her office, I know to race ahead and hit the desk to await my treats. I'm also renowned for my ability to clean off a desk or nightstand with the swipe of a paw. Imagine the clutter if it weren't for me.

As highly intelligent readers, you surely now realize that I am the most special creature in our household—if not in the universe. Perhaps one day you too will be lucky enough to be owned by a calico cat.

Tinker the Wonder Dog as Told by Tinker

The view from Doggie Heaven has been pretty entertaining lately. I don't usually let earthly goings-on distract me, but Banjo and Puddin' thinking they're writers has gotten my attention. It seems Mum's gotten so lazy these days that she's letting Banjo and Puddin' tell their own stories. Well, no way Tinker the Wonder Dog is getting left out of the fun.

I'm not sure I can bring myself to refer to those two as Lord Banjo and Princess Puddin', no matter how special they think they are. They seem to have forgotten that I was the favorite child and that they were simply also-rans. I know that if I hadn't left for Doggie Heaven, they wouldn't be getting nearly as much attention. Sure, Banjo would get to go on walks with Dad and me, but that would be about it.

What kind of dog is Banjo anyway? He mostly just lies around or bugs Mum and Dad to pet him. He doesn't play with squeaky toys or stuffed animals. And never mind balls; he won't even pick one up.

In my prime, I chased balls pretty much nonstop. It was usually Dad who quit first, when his pitching arm went out, though every once in a while I had to lie down to rest—with a ball in my mouth, of course. If I couldn't get anyone to play with me, I'd find something to play with in one of my toy boxes. Well, if I'm honest, I sometimes pulled out quite a few toys until I got just the right one, and I never did learn to put them away.

I had a football, a beach ball, a Mickey Mouse ball, and loads of racquet and tennis balls. If Mum sat down on the floor to work out with her medicine ball, I'd try to grab that. And when on my own in the backyard without a playmate, I'd play nose ball. That's what Mum and Dad called the game I played by bouncing a ball up a tree with my nose and catching it on the way down.

When we were stuck inside, Mum and Dad would sit on the floor with me and play roller ball. Have you ever rolled a tennis ball to a dog who could stop it with a paw and then use her nose to roll it back your way? Yup, that's how we played ball in the house. Mum let me and Dad get a bit more rambunctious on the screened porch, where the toy box was filled with balls and squeaky toys. Sometimes we played ball; sometimes we played with squeaky toys. Dad squeaked and tossed them, and I caught 'em—usually in midair.

I did slow down a bit my last few years, but if you were a fourteen-year-old dog, you'd slow down too. I was no longer leaping in the air to catch toys and balls, nor running nonstop to retrieve them in the backyard, but I was still a star at rolling a ball and demolishing stuffed animals.

I hate to brag, not being royal and all, but I was pretty talented, and certainly more entertaining than Lord Banjo. And Dad always called me Tinker, my little girl with the pretty curl. It's clear I was well loved. I may not be able to beat Princess Puddin's acrobatics, but hey, she's just a cat, so she was never really in the running for top dog.

Now, enough of this writing thing. It's time to get back to chasing balls through the woods and splashing in the Doggie Heaven creek. It's not that I don't miss you, Mum and Dad, but life is pretty darned good here in Doggie Heaven.

Chapter 3

Summer Sojourns

My favorite season of the year is winter, preferably accompanied by snow and frigid temperatures. The summers I merely endure, and you can most often find me in my royal reclining position in the coolest spot in the house, but this summer was different. Perhaps because of my newly minted status as a Royal Dog, the Royal Parents and the Royal Critter Sitter saw to it that summer was one big adventure for Lord Banjo.

Hot town, summer in the city—that's Hotlanta. Those Lovin' Spoonful lyrics describe my Royal City perfectly. Atlanta is *hot*, *hot*, *hot*. When you have long, thick, black fur, like mine, the heat is oppressive, and your belly absorbs it from the pavement. So, what do the Royal Parents do about my miserable state? Do they send me north to summer camp in Minnesota or Maine, or maybe even Canada? Do they provide me a pool so I can cool off with frequent dips? Do they turn the air conditioner to the fifties? No!

They take a two-week vacation to Europe and send me to Miss Beverly's summer camp. Where? In a suburb of the Royal City, where it's not any cooler than it is at the Royal Abode. Mum and Dad take off to cruise the Danube where they have to bundle up against the chill, and they leave me behind in the hot, humid, urban—well, okay, *suburban*—jungle. Is that any way to treat Lord Banjo?

When Mum and Dad bathed and brushed me, dressed me in a sporty new bandana, and loaded me and my food into the car, I knew something was up. I was anticipating a trip to the mountains, one of my favorite spots. And when we pulled up to Miss Beverly's, I figured she was joining us because she and I both like mountain vacations. Imagine my surprise when Mum and Dad drove off without either of us. I barked, "Hey, aren't you forgetting somebody?"

I began to get over my dismay when Miss Beverly knelt down, hugged my neck, and cooed, "We're gonna have a big time, Lord Banjo. Welcome to summer camp!" And as soon as it cooled off a bit, she took me on a walk around her little town.

The first time I visited Miss Beverly, it was quiet, but in the summer, her town is abuzz with activity. And dogs! There were dogs everywhere—walking, lounging on the grass in the town square, and resting beneath tables in outdoor cafés while their people had coffee and cocktails. This town is definitely dog crazy. Lucky me, either Miss Beverly or Camp Counselor SarahAnne took me on two walks a day.

Those two kept me busy, sometimes to the point of exhaustion. Truthfully, *always* to the point of exhaustion. Between walks, I spent my time lying on the cool wood floor in the den—positioned beneath the ceiling fan *and* in front of a floor fan.

Since it was Miss Beverly who first suggested—more like *demanded*—I go on a diet, you won't be surprised to hear that she saw summer camp as her opportunity to ramp up my weight loss—as though I weren't already starving at home on my ridiculously reduced rations.

To take my mind off my hunger pangs and my close encounters with heatstroke, I sent Mum e-mails about all my camp activities. Am I not a wonderful son?

Day One

Dear Mum,

Miss Beverly and I walked our two miles tonight through the busy town square, which was jam-packed with people and pups sitting, strolling, and just hanging out waiting for the *huge* lantern parade. We were just in time to claim a prime viewing seat on the corner for the start of the parade.

I behaved like the Royal Dog I am. I waited patiently for the parade to begin and watched the whole thing without fidgeting. I've never been a nervous dog, and nothing much scares me. The parade was a sight to behold, especially all the colorful lanterns. But best of all, I got lots of hugs. Honestly, I think some of the kids may have enjoyed *me* more than the parade. Those toy humans *do* love to throw their arms around my neck and rub my back.

Love,

Your Boy, Lord Banjo

Day Three

Dear Mum,

Early this morning found Miss Beverly and me strolling the local college campus where folks were getting ready for the afternoon graduation ceremony. Then I headed home to *thud*, as you say.

As part of our evening walk, we took in a concert on the square. This town is a happening place. And I met a good-looking dog named Lola. She was a cute gray-and-white thing—*très jolie*, as the French say—and she flirted with me and even asked, "What's your name, big fella?"

"Lord Banjo," I replied proudly.

"Oh, *Lord* Banjo." She sniffed, "You must think you're too good to hang with us common pups."

We barked to each other some more, and I had her convinced I was a cool dude until she asked where I lived. My answer was the kiss of death.

"I live across town, but I'm here at summer camp for two weeks."

"That's it, you're geographically undesirable," Lola pronounced, and she turned away.

And that was the end of what could've been a beautiful romance. Miss Beverly saw that I was dejected, so she took me home and fed me ice cubes, which made me feel a little better.

I'm still pouting and panting and trying my best to recover from this miserable heat and humidity so I can be perky tomorrow morning. That's supposed to be the coolest morning yet, so I should be happier. This heat is just too much for a little boy in a fuzzy suit, as Dad says.

I am not, however, allowing the heat to dampen my appetite. I'm eating with gusto—all two niblets Miss Beverly allows me. I'll be heading straight for Puddin's dabs of wet food when I get home. That reminds me, just who is cleaning Puddin's bowl while I'm away?

Hope you and Dad are having fun. Bring me a T-shirt, preferably one with a royal crest on it.

Love,

Your Beautiful Boy, Lord Banjo

Dear son,

Sounds like you're enjoying summer camp and being a good boy. I'm so sorry Lola dissed you, but you're better off without a Debbie Downer dog. A parade and a concert all in one weekend! That's special.

It's been cool and wet here, just your kind of weather.

Love you!

Day Five

Dear Mum,

Please pay attention—I am OMG starving. The shiny finish is gone from my bowl because I've been licking it so much. Miss Beverly bought me a can of some delicious food, and she puts a teeny dollop on my dry food and mixes it in to make me think I'm getting a large bowl of wet food. It's yummy, smells just like grilled steak, and tastes even better, but she's not fooling me—*I'm still starving!*

I just returned from my seventh two-mile walk, but tonight I jogged. Seriously, I *jogged* because it was such a cool day. Miss Beverly brushed me too, and lots of people commented on my fabulous fur coat. Quite a few asked if I was a Newfoundland, whatever that is. Miss Beverly says that's because Newfoundlands are black like me. Some silly kid asked if I was a wolf, and I growled at her. Just kidding, Mum, you know I'd never be mean to *anyone*.

I've been sleeping in Camp Counselor SarahAnne's room because she has a floor fan in there aimed right at me. It's cool to sleep in a girly room. She's decorated it in purples and lavenders, and I especially like the sheer purple cloth draped over the head of her bed. I think this must be what a royal bedroom looked like back in the day—you know, when the Sun King ruled France, and my ancestors roamed the court. Everyone knows only royalty could use the color purple. Come to think of it, I think it's only fitting that you find me a royal purple bed for my bedroom at home.

Today, Mr. John had a bonsai workshop in the backyard, and I lay around receiving lots of belly rubs as I surveyed everyone's work. There's so much to do and see around here. Why don't we have this kind of entertainment at the Royal Abode? Dad's good at taking care of the herd of bicycles in the garage; maybe he could do a bicycle-repair or leaf-blowing workshop. We need more adoring visitors—adoring of *me*.

But back to the most important point: did I mention I'm starving? You need to buy my T-shirt a size smaller.

Barely Hanging On,

Lord Banjo

Dear son,

Do please remember that Miss Beverly doubles as the Royal Physician and is only doing what's best for you.

I suppose it's not a good time to mention all the varieties of sausage we've sampled as we've traveled throughout Germany and Austria.

We miss you and Puddin' terribly. We haven't seen many dogs here, which seems odd, and not a single cat.

I think your stay with Miss Beverly sounds like a stay at a resort, maybe like Canyon Ranch Spa, complete with the hunger pangs. So Miss Beverly brushed you. What's next? A massage? Yoga?

Love,

Mum

Day Seven

Dear Mum,

It's the *good*, the *bad*, and the *ugly*—well nothing really *ugly*, that just sounded cool. Please know that despite my severe food deprivation, this camp is working out for me.

It's nice being the only furball in the house. I get so much attention without my calico sister demanding Dad swing that crazy bird toy for her. On my second walk yesterday, we explored the cemetery, where I waded in the creek. The water was up to my shoulders in one spot. Miss Beverly didn't even fuss about me being a little muddy and promised we could do it again later this week.

I barked once this morning—just one big bark. It crept out of my mouth without warning and startled me and everyone else. I'm not sure what came over me; it may have been my disappointment when I realized it was raining and we weren't going for our morning walk. You know I hate to miss a walk, especially in a cool rain, but I could tell Miss Beverly wasn't going out in that weather. Though it is my royal prerogative to bark whenever the mood strikes, I don't think I'll do it again anytime soon, because the camp officials didn't seem too thrilled.

Now for the *bad*: I have been banned from *all* bedrooms. Seems that I have awakened Camp Counselor SarahAnne in the wee hours with my flopping around on the floor. She claims I made her bed shake. Who does that sound like, even if she didn't use the word *thud*? Maybe when I waste away to nothing, I can return. I am taking my banishment in stride, as I have several other favorite spots, including the tile floor in the kitchen.

Getting excited about my T-shirt and wondering whether they make edible ones over there. I'm dreaming of one that tastes like a grilled steak. Be on the lookout.

Love,

Your Big Boy, Banjo—maybe not so big anymore!

Dear son,

When I read *the good, the bad, and the ugly*, I was worried you'd been sick in Miss Beverly's house. Glad that wasn't the case. I guess flopping around on a wood floor is noisier than doing it in your carpeted Royal Bedroom, and you must have disturbed the Camp Counselor's beauty sleep. You know those college kids need lots of rest.

I'm glad you're not barking, but can you explain why you bark at home and not at camp? Your creek adventure sounds fun and refreshing. Not sure about an edible T-shirt. Maybe a Bavarian collar from Austria?

Great Norwegian salmon last night for dinner, and then vanilla ice cream for dessert. Your dad had a banana split today with his lunch! Oh, sorry, guess you don't want to hear about our desserts!

Love,
The Royal Mum

Day Nine

Dear Mum,

Proud, proud, proud. You should be *proud* of me. I was the champion walker today, and I'm starting to get into shape.

Today marked my *thirty-fifth* mile since you checked me into this torture facility, and I trotted the whole time, leaving Miss Beverly hanging on for dear life. We just returned from our evening walk through the square, where the crowds were listening to music and dining outside, and about half of them wanted to run their fingers through my beautiful royal fur.

But the best part was the fantastic job I did snagging a discarded hamburger bun lying on the sidewalk. I was *fast*, and about two minutes later I spied another one. At first, I thought it was a rock disguised as a bun, but it was the real thing. Miss Beverly was none too pleased. I think she's going to make me suffer for my behavior by reducing my rations from two niblets to one!

But now to the most exciting part. I saw Puddin' today. It had to be Puddin', because this calico kitty had a white belly just like hers and a gold patch between her eyes. She was sitting there at the end of a long ramp. I was anxious to get close to her, but Miss Beverly wouldn't let me run up the ramp, so I sat down . . . and Puddin' sat down . . . and we tried to outstare each other.

We looked like little Buddhas. Don't misunderstand that Buddha comment—

no way I have a Buddha belly—but I was very, very still. That went on for about five minutes. Miss Beverly kept trying to get me to move on, but I wasn't having it, and you know when I don't want to move, I'm immovable. It was definitely Puddin', I'm telling you, but she stuck her little pink nose in the air and turned away, so that was the end of that.

I mean, I don't want you to think I miss the little calico furball. I'm enjoying the break and all the individual attention I'm getting.

It's past my bedtime now, so I'm going to stretch out for my royal rest in preparation for tomorrow's walk. Have you found my edible T-shirt yet? I may want matching pants too. I can already taste my steak-flavored, edible T-shirt and pants.

>Your Best Boy,
>Big Bad Banjo, the Royal Pooch

Dear son,

I *am* proud! Except of course of your bun escapade. Tsk, tsk. I am sure you'll pay for that. I know you're growing more and more fond of Miss Beverly, but I hope you haven't forgotten your mum and dad.

I think you may *really* miss Puddin', or the calico furball, as you call her, since you *imagined* you saw her!

We were excited today because we saw a dog who could be your German cousin. He was in a courtyard sheltering from the rain, but he looked as though he enjoyed the cold and wet as much as you do. Maybe some of the Royal Dogs of France were sent to Germany. The raindrops were standing on his fur, making him all shiny, just like you look after a walk in the rain.

Love you and miss you!
Mum and Dad

Day Eleven

Dear Mum,

First, let me say I did not *imagine* seeing Puddin'. When the Royal Pooch says he saw something, he did.

Now, for the big announcement: *Dah-dahdah-dah!* Can you hear the Royal Trumpeters proclaiming the news? I *did* it; I'm the Big Loser! As of today, I've lost three pounds. That's a lot when you start at seventy-eight. Miss Beverly wants to know why I only lost two pounds in six weeks with you and Dad, but three pounds in two weeks at summer camp. Even I know the answer to that question! She's been starving me!

Hurry home before I evaporate.

Love,

Your Skinny Royal Boy

Dear son,

We are anxiously awaiting our taxi to the airport. Dad is looking forward to plying you with treats, but don't tell Miss Beverly! The truth is that all three of us will be on starvation diets for the next few weeks, especially the Royal Dad. You may be Lord Banjo, but Dad is the Pancake King or the Dessert King, depending on the time of day!

Love,

Mum and Dad

Ah, home, sweet home. I'm delighted to be back with Mum, Dad, and even Princess Puddin'. As usual, the princess made us call and call and search for her before she chose to grace us with her presence. She just suddenly appears, and then all is well. She stays hidden long enough to let us know she is mightily displeased with being left on her own, but she's all over Mum and Dad after she makes her point. Too bad for her that Miss Beverly's summer camp doesn't accept cats.

Mum and Dad have showered me with attention and affection, as well they should after a two-week absence. Lucky for them, I don't hold a grudge. And I must say that getting to stay with Miss Beverly is far better than staying at the kennel they used to send me to—except that at the kennel, they don't starve me. I admit that the belly rubs, walks, and adoring fans *do* make up somewhat for the diet, but there's no need to share that bit of information with the Royal Parents.

Lord Banjo is pleased to be back at the Royal Abode, except for the vet visit he had to endure upon his return. Read more about this nasty turn of events in my thank-you note to Miss Beverly.

Dear Miss Beverly and Camp Counselor SarahAnne,

Thank you so much for a wonderful summer camp experience. Where do I begin? Here at home, I don't get to go to parades and concerts like you have in your town, so those events were special treats for me. I also don't get to wade in creeks, except occasionally when Mum and Dad take me to the mountains, and I don't usually go on walks twice a day.

At home, Dad walks me up and down our street and we see other dogs and their parents, but I just don't get the oohs and aahs and lots of people wanting to touch me like I do at summer camp. Do you think that means the folks in your neck of the woods are just more appreciative of my royal status?

Thanks too for giving me a bath so I had a fresh, minty smell to my coat. That made it easier for Mum and Dad to hug me, and I'm so glad, because I really did miss them. I must tell you, though, that I was ready to run back to camp when Mum took me to the vet. Even though you took such good care of me, there was just no avoiding those hot spots that I get every spring and summer. The vet said she'd seen lots of poor doggies like me, itching and scratching all over.

I couldn't believe my ears when she said, "If you want to attack this aggressively and you're willing to put up with Lord Banjo having a baboon butt, then we'll shave him, clean him up, and give him a shot." Worse yet, Mum said yes. No one asked me! Do they not realize that Royal Dogs get to make these kinds of decisions for themselves? Yes, I feel better, and I'm not scratching and chewing nearly as much, but still, the embarrassment is unbearable.

Oh well, this too shall pass. Meanwhile, I'm showing off the new trick the camp counselor taught me: I'm shaking everyone's hand with my royal paw, and my subjects are in awe of my skill. Mum and Dad are also super impressed with the spring in my step on our walks. Dad even got up this morning at 7:15 to walk me two miles. And oh yes, I'm still hungry. Apparently, it was a mistake for me to write Mum and Dad that I'd lost three pounds. They are now determined to follow the summer camp a.k.a. boot camp diet plan until I lose *five more pounds*. Thank goodness I'm home with Puddin' and can lick dabs of food from her bowl when she's not looking.

Despite the starvation diet you insisted on, I'd really like to come back sometime. I hope you'll be offering a fall camp when Mum and Dad go away again. I promise to be good as gold. And I sure hope my bald spot has grown back in, so my many admiring subjects won't be disappointed.

Much love,

Your Favorite Camper, Lord Banjo

(I am the favorite, right?)

Dear Lord Banjo,

We are happy to hear you enjoyed your experience with us, and we are delighted to provide your summer camp report card.

Camp Counselor SarahAnne reports, "You are one of the best campers we've ever had! We are very glad to hear the rump itch is being treated! Sometimes you can pick up weird itches at camp. I look forward to seeing a picture of this new 'baboon do' you have, and I'm glad it's giving you some relief!

"We miss having a doggie to walk. The creek walk isn't as fun without you, but we are very glad to hear your dad is keeping up the royal regimen and taking you on fun morning walks. Can't wait to see you again soon and give you lots of kisses."

And I, Miss Beverly, concur. You are a great houseguest. You didn't make sounds other than the *thud* of collapsing onto the floor and the sloppy slurps as you inhaled water. You were kind to everyone you met, even the commoners. You never demanded a thing. You wear your royalty well.

Your fall reservation is confirmed, Your Highness.

Sincerely,

Miss Beverly

It's midsummer, and the royal diet plan is paying off; I'm fast approaching my goal weight. Sounds like Weight Watchers, doesn't it? I don't attend weekly meetings, but I sure stick to my diet and exercise routine.

My torture plan—I mean diet plan—started in late winter when I weighed in at eighty pounds. I had only lost two pounds by mid-May when I went to summer camp. There Miss Beverly, a.k.a. the Royal Physician, cut my rations, and I lost three more pounds.

Miss Beverly walked me every day, sometimes twice a day, and my dad took over that regimen when I returned home. I think all these walks have been more about Dad wanting to lose the weight he gained on vacation than it's been any concern for me, but whatever the inspiration, I'm getting plenty of walks.

It's been so hot here that Dad has started getting up early, as in 6:00 or 6:30 a.m., to get in a walk before the heat sets in. I have to say that he and I have disagreed a few times as to what constitutes real *heat*. He may call me his little boy in the fuzzy suit, but he doesn't seem to get what that means for me in hot, muggy weather. Even worse, he's lately been trying to squeeze in *three* walks a day.

Sometimes, when he gets out the leash, sunglasses, and ball cap, I refuse to go to the door and look at him as though he's crazy. Well, truthfully, I believe he *is* crazy to think I'm going out in that weather. He gets a tad irritated and goes without me, which is more than fine by me. Soon enough,

Mum comes downstairs, and we sit on the screened porch under the overhead fan. Even that can be much too hot, but I'm a little trooper. Some might say I'm a *big* trooper.

For a short time, we made regular visits to a new fountain at the entrance to a nearby gated community. Now, that was seriously cool. I could stand in water up to my royal belly and walk under the spray too. Mum wondered when the homeowners were going to notice and ban us. Not to worry, we struck wading off our list when the water started turning green, a situation I'm sure had nothing to do with me. Had the drain been blocked with beautiful, wavy, black hair, that would've been a different story.

Dad has also accused me of *balking*. He claims that I just stop midwalk and refuse to go any farther. Since there are no additional witnesses, I say it's his word against mine. On the other hand, it's worth noting that I'm no dummy. When he decides to walk in 98 percent humidity and eighty-five- to ninety-five-degree heat, someone needs to take control and be sure neither of us has heatstroke.

And now, drumroll please, the news about my weight: I'm a mean, lean fighting machine, weighing in at seventy-two pounds! You'd think that would mean an ice cream and cake celebration, right? Apparently not. The Royal Physician says I have another two pounds to go, so the Royal Ps—Physician and Parents—have decided *not* to increase my rations beyond my meager two cups a day.

I'm looking for somewhere to hide that darned measuring cup. Meanwhile, I remain committed to keeping Puddin's dish licked clean. My vigilance should keep Jelly Belly from getting any bigger. Cute nickname, right? Can't you tell I'm all about brotherly love?

I thought I wouldn't go back to camp until the fall, but Mum and Dad took another summer trip without me, so I was dropped off at Miss Beverly's for a long weekend. I was sad when Mum and Dad first left, but soon got back into the swing of things with Miss Beverly and my many loyal subjects.

Once again, I'm sharing my camp communications to the Royal Parents, and I'm also sharing two of Miss Beverly's e-mails to them. My exercise regimen with the Royal Dad is paying off, and it seems I caught Miss Beverly off guard with my newfound energy. Her take on our first walk is LOL funny, though I see no humor in her final email, where she once again rants about my royal figure. You be the judge.

Dear Royal Clients,

Forget this getting-in-shape stuff! The new leaner, meaner Banjo Boy is killin' me! He whined when he caught sight of me grabbing for the leash this morning, and he ran to the back door. When I opened it, he was down the steps in a flash—Banjo, flash, mind you. Then we were off to the races! No just lazily walking for this boy. For fifty minutes—and I know the precise number because I gasped through each one of them—he trotted while I sprinted and stumbled to keep up.

The temps weren't bad, but the humidity was 82 percent. I passed a neighbor on her way to Friday-morning exercise class as Banjo and I approached the home stretch, and she had the audacity to ask if I were going to the class. Guess she missed my beet-red face, labored breathing, and the sweat pouring off my body.

Banjo is recovering with both a ceiling fan and floor fan blowing on him. Me? I may never recover.

Sincerely,
Miss Beverly

Dear Mum and Dad,

Mark it on the calendar! I *galloped*! Not a fast walk, not a trot, a *gallop*. It wasn't that far, just the length of the kitchen. I was so excited to head out for another walk, I couldn't contain myself. Miss Beverly, for some reason, was not all that excited about another wild ride. I could tell she was relieved that my adoring admirers slowed our pace to a crawl as we traversed the town square. We couldn't get more than, let's say, ten yards before someone would stop us to inquire about my heritage or my name and, oh Lordy, those tiny toy humans just couldn't stop themselves from throwing their arms around my neck and smothering their little faces in my fur. The mothers could be heard crying, "Just *pet* the doggie," but the kids ignored them, which was fine by me.

We escaped the crowds long enough to get in a brisk walk through a nearby neighborhood, only to be stopped by two older couples on our return trip through the square. They were dining together outside a restaurant and had a pair of starter dogs who enjoyed crawling under and over me. One of the gentlemen demonstrated his intelligence by asking if I was a Great Pyrenees mix. The waitress who brought their food exclaimed over me too, and insisted on going inside and bringing me a treat, and believe it or not, Miss Beverly allowed me to have it. Friday night in Miss Beverly's town is the *bomb*!

Love,

Your Royal Boy, Banjo

Dear Mum and Dad,

The Royal Physician, a.k.a. Miss Beverly, has gotten all serious and is declaring I need to lose *more* weight. I'm in such good shape I wore her out, and yet she thinks I need to slim down further? I thought for sure that once she saw me back at camp, she'd change her mind about the extra two pounds. Her notes claim that we *agree* on this course of action. *Do not* believe a word.

She rudely mentions chest fat. I believe she fails to realize that my breed boasts a massive chest, and as a fine male specimen, I have a massive, *manly* chest.

Is there no end to this madness? I think this latest declaration is payback for me wearing her out the first morning. Please take her report with a *big* grain of salt.

Notes from the Royal Physician:

Lord Banjo arrived yesterday at our clinic for his three-month evaluation. I am happy to report that he looks much more fit to rule, and he indicates that he indeed feels better. However, we agree that there is more to accomplish.

He needs to slim down two more pounds by the time he is reevaluated in our location next month. The loss of these two pounds should help reduce the *chest fat* that is still a bit worrisome. To accomplish this goal, we need to limit his daily food intake to a scant two cups with one low-calorie treat in the early afternoon. Daily exercise should continue but should be of short duration while the heat and humidity remain high.

If I may be of further assistance, please call my office.

Sincerely,

The Royal Physician

PS: He seems to think his diet should include dabs of cat food. What's up with that?

What do you picture when you hear the phrase "dog days of summer"? I, the Royal Pooch, envision hound dogs lying on dusty, sagging wooden porches and their people sitting in rockers alongside them. I see straw hats, ice-cold lemonade, and maybe a corn-cob pipe and overalls à la *The Beverly Hillbillies*.

Lucky for me, I don't have to sack out on a hot porch; I get to recline inside anywhere I choose—well, except on the furniture. Imagine my surprise when Mum shared with me the origins of the phrase.

It dates back to the ancient Greeks and refers to the dog star, Sirius, and the time of the year when it looks as though the star rises before the sun, typically in late July. Just as it is here in Georgia, July and August are awfully hot in Greece. The ancient Greeks and Romans believed this to be the time of year when fevers and catastrophes were prevalent. I guess either the dog star or the heat can make people crazy. Us dogs? I think it only makes us lazy.

If you want to get technical, the dog days *do* shift around and aren't always in July, but why ruin a good story? To me, it's enough that the dog days are somehow associated with dogs, whether it's a star or me, and it makes sense to lie still in the shade.

To my dad, this dog-star information is meaningless. He's still taking me for walks not only in the cool of the morning, but also in the heat of the day around lunchtime. His behavior brings to mind the lyrics of the Noël Coward song "Mad Dogs and Englishmen." That song explains that those born in the tropics are smart enough to stay inside in the heat of the day, but for some strange reason, Englishmen go out and about as do, as the song says, mad dogs.

Suffice it to say that I am neither mad nor English. I'm French, remember? Come to think of it, Dad is neither a dog nor an Englishman, so what does that leave? Methinks he may be mad.

The Royal Mum, on the other hand, is Greek and believes wholeheartedly in siestas, as do her countrymen. Thank goodness for small favors. When I can make it up the stairs after my midday workout with Dad, you can find me lying next to Mum's bed in front of the fan, or better yet, holding down the tile floor in the Royal Bathroom—always the coolest spot in the house. Both Royal Mums and Royal Dogs know how to behave during the dog days.

I may be Lord Banjo, but my aristocratic heritage doesn't mean I'm stuck up or demanding. Perhaps I'm a teensy bit demanding when it comes to belly rubs, but that's it.

These past few days, though, have tried my royal patience. You know I'm accustomed to taking a morning walk, whether it's at home with Dad or at camp with Miss Beverly, so I was disappointed one morning when Dad failed to get up early enough for our walk.

I have a forgiving nature and thought, *Oh well, I can miss one hot morning; I'm sure Dad will get up earlier tomorrow*, and I quickly got over my disappointment when Mum put me in her car. I was sure we were going somewhere special for a walk and was hoping it was the river.

When we pulled up at the Royal Groomer's, it clicked. "Uh-oh," I groaned, "another bath." It's not that I mind being clean and shiny. I just don't particularly care for the bathing process. If only someone could come up with a way for me to get clean by playing in the rain or wading in a creek, two of my favorite activities.

I consoled myself with the knowledge that I'd soon be home getting lots of kisses and hugs, but *no*, there was another surprise to come. It seemed a good idea when the Royal Mum asked the groomer to trim the long, scraggly hairs around my ever-shrinking tummy so as to show off my manly chest and trim waist. Unfortunately, that request got lost in translation, and I've ended up with some kind of choppy do.

My lovely black-and-white chest looks as though a madman hacked my fur coat with dull scissors. I know it will grow back, but it's terribly embarrassing—especially when I roll over for a belly rub.

I figured the week could only get better, but again the next day, no walk. *What's up with this?* I wondered. There was also no water in my water bowl. Things were getting stranger by the minute, but I'm an even-keeled kind of boy, and I got excited when Dad loaded me in his car. Except once again, no ride to the river. This time, it was a ride to see the Royal Dentist. What next?

The dentist knocked me out and cleaned my teeth. When Dad picked me up, I was woozy and had a sore mouth. I could barely eat that night or the next morning, and I was beginning to think Mum and Dad had lost their minds. I could only think that I needed to get a message to the Royal Physician before my parents came up with yet another way to torture me.

Fortunately, before I could send out an SOS, I had a *pleasant* surprise: Mum's cousin arrived at the Royal Abode. That wise lady adores me, as do most folks, and she appropriately showered me with hugs and belly rubs. She even accompanied Dad and me on our walks and let me sleep beside her bed.

I deserted the Royal Parents for two nights, only heading to their bedroom in time to wake them up, and I tried to get in the car to leave with Mum's cousin, just to make a point. What point? Mum and Dad need to mend their ways. Much as I would hate to leave them, I have plenty of admirers out there who would take me in should there be a repeat of last week's events.

The good news is the royal routine has resumed, and all is once again right in the world. Ah yes, the Royal Pooch is mightily pleased.

I joined the Royal Parents and Miss Beverly on a trip to the mountains for Labor Day weekend. I *do* love it there. We stay in an ancient, rustic cabin, where I can smell the outdoors even when I'm indoors. And then there's the porch, with rockers perfectly positioned so that everyone can rub my belly.

With people coming and going nonstop, I get lots of attention, whether it's on the porch or sitting around inside in front of the massive fireplace, and I generously share the love by going from person to person so that everyone has an opportunity to pet me. The best part was when the dinner bell rang, and the crowd gathered around the table for dinner. Guess what they forgot? The appetizers on the coffee table. I had almost gulped down all the guacamole and chips before Mum heard the chomping noises and leaped up to grab the goodies.

In addition to lounging around, at least once a day we go down the hill to walk around the lake, where I find plenty of enticing smells and occasionally some picnic delicacies left behind. My walkers are pretty vigilant, so I've yet to do more than sniff the food I find.

Dad and I walked together the first few days, and then he and Mum left me with Miss Beverly while they went off on yet another trip. I'm sure you've figured out by now that they are a well-traveled pair. Miss Beverly and I stayed at the lake a few extra days and had a grand time without them before heading back to town.

Now for the *good*, the *bad*, and the *fantastic*. First up, let's get the *bad* out of the way. I was doing the lake walk with Miss Beverly, and it was just too much for me—the sun reflecting off the sparkling blue water of the lake and that mischievous goose who took flight right in front of my nose! My instincts took over, and I couldn't help myself. I took off behind the goose with Miss Beverly hanging on for dear life. As I chased that bird farther into the lake, Miss Beverly sat on her haunches trying to anchor herself to the shore, but that tactic didn't work all that well. I pulled her right into the lake, like a boat pulling a skier.

She finally came to a halt when the water reached her knees. I didn't get that goose, but I *did* get some applause from a small group of spectators who had gathered to watch the show. Fortunately for me, Miss Beverly wasn't angry. She laughed as she pulled me out, and since her shoes were already wet and muddy, she waded right back in and held on to the tip of the long leash, so I could swim back and forth parallel to the shore. It felt like heaven.

Now for the *good*. I slept quietly upstairs in the loft beside Miss Beverly's bed without disturbing anyone. We visited Miss Beverly's cousins in another cabin, and I behaved like a perfect prince, in keeping with my royal breeding. And on the van ride back to the Royal City, I was so quiet that Miss Beverly stopped to check in the very back to make sure she hadn't forgotten me. Since then, I've continued to be as good as gold in every way, and I'm pretty sure I've redeemed myself for the lake escapade.

Finally, wait until you hear the *fantastic*. Back at Miss Beverly's, I've been prancing on my walks around the town square, and I must look handsome, because I regularly hear "What a beautiful dog." The supreme compliment came from Camp Counselor SarahAnne. When I greeted her at the door, her eyes widened, and she exclaimed, "Banjo, you look so good, and you're so thin!" SarahAnne's words made my day, but there was more to come.

Sound the trumpets! Miss Beverly took me to weigh in, and I've lost my final two pounds to reach my goal weight of seventy! I'm getting used to the new me and plan to pursue a modeling career. I'm aiming to make the centerfold for *Canine*

Playboy. Then, a career as a personal trainer could be in the cards. I can see it now: a chain of fitness centers called "Bodacious Bodies by Banjo." With my svelte new figure, the sky's the limit.

Chapter 4

A Royal Holiday Season

November kicks off my favorite time of the year, not only because the weather turns cooler, but also because the holidays arrive. Family and friends celebrate in style, and my royal presence is much in demand.

I had reservations at a local kennel for Thanksgiving, but Miss Beverly had a cancellation and invited me to spend the holiday with her. I was looking forward to my visit when I got the best-ever invitation from Camp Counselor SarahAnne:

Hi Lord Banjo,

My roommates and I are wondering if you'd like to visit us at our new camp location this Tuesday when your parents are out of town. We'd like to have you as our guest for one night before you spend the rest of your holiday with Miss Beverly. We're having a Thanksgiving dinner at our house that night with lots of our friends—Friendsgiving—and we think you would be an excellent addition to our celebration!

Please let me know if you are interested in visiting us.

Love,

Camp Counselor SarahAnne

PS: Please tell your sister Puddin' she is welcome to visit another time.

Dear Camp Counselor SarahAnne,

How delightful! My favorite camp counselor is having a party, and I'm the guest of honor? I know you didn't exactly say that, but I bet I'm the only four-legged royal guest you're inviting.

I accept your invitation with pleasure. How very cool! I see a new crowd of admirers in my future. I had a bath yesterday, and I'm ready to be seen and touched and hugged. I do hope my green bandana will be a hit.

BTW, silly girl, I am not mentioning this to Puddin'. She'd be jealous, even though she's not very good with crowds.

I guess her colorful gold-and-brown-and-white coat is more appropriate for this holiday, but her behavior is not. But then, not all animals are as royally well behaved as I.

Sincerely,

Lord Banjo

Dear Lord Banjo,

Yay! We can't wait to see you! You will most definitely be the guest of honor,

and my roommates and all our guests
are looking forward to meeting you.

> Yippee,
>
> Camp Counselor SarahAnne

With the invitation extended and accepted, the Royal Parents dropped me off, and I was the main attraction. I think the picture of me in my pilgrim hat may be one of my best.

Upon my arrival, my hosts walked me *three* times, once through the lively local park. It was a beautiful fall day, and I had a grand time.

Once the party was in full swing, I couldn't believe my good fortune. Everyone wanted to pet me. They must have all heard that Lord Banjo would be in attendance. As I wandered from guest to guest, I enjoyed belly rubs, ear scratches, exclamations about how handsome I was—you name it. I did manage to snag a few licks of dip, but the partygoers were pretty careful about keeping their goodies out of reach of my tongue.

When the last guests left in the wee hours, I crashed and didn't open my eyes until lunchtime the next day. I must say that spending time with a bunch of energetic Millennials is pretty cool, even though it took me a day to recover.

Mais oui! Can you see me doing a paw pump? It was twenty-seven degrees this morning, and I finally got to take a morning walk in my kind of weather. Forget packages beneath the tree; just give me nonstop chilly days. I pranced, I tell you, I pranced. I wish someone had videotaped my walk, as I just know the wind was ruffling my royal black fur, and I looked majestic with my head held high.

The Royal Dad, of course, was all bundled up and complaining of the chill. We even saw some munchkin doggies out in their cute little coats. Lord Banjo does not require a coat. We Great Pyrenees have natural coats perfect for the cold.

I could have taken a longer walk, but Dad was eager to get home. As we hit the front porch, he gathered a load of kindling and bustled inside to start a fire in the wood-burning stove. Only after the fire was going did he take off his heavy jacket and gloves. I find the cold invigorating, so on days like this, you can find me lying by the front door as far from the fire as possible.

Now that I've completed my brisk walk, inspected the neighborhood, and determined my people are in no imminent danger, I'm ready to fulfill my watchdog duties for the rest of the day from indoors. These duties I can handle from a reclining position while surveying the yard through the glass door. With a gentle growl, I've already alerted Dad to a few rogue walkers. Truth be told, I've also alerted him to a few falling leaves. It's a tough job, but someone has to do it.

As I lie here, I'm pondering how to inspire Dad to take me out for a late afternoon walk. Since he's talking about needing a new pair of long underwear, I'm not holding out much hope for walk number two today.

We were all ready to head out for our Christmas vacation. The suitcases were in the car, and I was loaded snugly in next to them. I wasn't sure where we were going, but I'm never picky, so I settled down for the drive.

The car came to a stop only a few miles from home, and what to my wondering eyes should appear? I can assure you it was neither a sleigh nor eight tiny reindeer. It wasn't even a stop at Miss Beverly's for a stay while Mum and Dad were out of town. Noooo. We pulled up at the kennel.

Yes, I've stayed here before for a night or two, but for five nights? How could they? Where was

Santa when Mum and Dad came up with this idea? I was certainly nice, not naughty, and did not deserve to be banished to stay with a crowd of *common* dogs. Harrumph!

When Mum and Dad finally came back to get me, Mum told me she had noticed me on the doggie cam doing lots of lying around while the other inmates—I mean dogs—wandered by, sniffed me, and went on to play amongst themselves. Naturally, that's what she saw. The commoners are always in awe of Lord Banjo, and he is rarely interested in joining in their foolish games.

You will recall that we Great Pyrenees are calm watchdogs. None of this mindless frolicking for us. I do enjoy the munchkin dogs leaping over me from time to time, but endless playing is not for me. Thank goodness Mum and Dad returned bearing gifts for Puddin' and me. I'm not letting on that I'm royally pleased with the red-and-white Christmas collar they brought me, but I do think it looks stunning with my fluffy black coat. Mum says I can wear it through New Year's Day before it's packed away for next year.

I much prefer my stylish collar to the silly rubber duckies Puddin' got for the water bowl. With some regular walks, nonstop belly rubs, and a few extra treats, the Royal Parents will soon be back in my good graces. Let's keep that a secret for now, though, okay?

It's been a very good year for Lord Banjo. I didn't use Ancestry.com, but I *did* discover my Great Pyrenees lineage. The history of the breed explains all my extraordinary traits: my calm demeanor, my regal bearing, my bark, my size; the facts are all there in the details about the Great Pyrenees and leave no doubt that I am *indeed* special. I could listen to Mum read my DNA results over and over, and just thinking about my family tree gives me a warm, fuzzy feeling.

Learning that my ancestors were the Royal Dogs of the French court has given me a whole new lease on life. The Royal Parents understand now that I'm not a lazy layabout; I'm a calm ruler. I don't bark for the heck of it; I bark to protect my flock. I'm not too heavy; I'm on the small side for a breed that is *very* large. I don't play with balls and toys because I'm much too dignified for such activities.

I also know I've been lucky to have Miss Beverly as my Royal Critter Sitter and Royal Physician. As torturous as it was to lose ten pounds, I am now, as Miss Beverly says, "more fit to rule." These days, I don't even miss the extra portions, and I continue to have a spring in my step. I know it's important for me to take care of myself, because my loyal subjects love me and count on me. Even Princess Puddin' would have to agree with that sentiment, though she may never admit it.

As for next year, I have big plans. In addition to my modeling career and my Bodacious Bodies by Banjo fitness centers, I have several more goals. First, I want to learn French! I know a few phrases, but as a Royal Dog of the French court, it behooves me to be more fluent in the language. Second, I hear rumors that the Royal Parents are planning a trip to France, and I think it only proper that I accompany them. I feel confident the French would welcome me with open arms—and belly rubs. Finally, I'd like to have a little four-legged brother or sister. The Royal Parents will take some convincing, but I plan to enlist Miss Beverly's support for the challenge. She helped them adopt Princess Puddin', and I'm sure she can find another worthy addition to the family.

Lest I forget, I'd love to write another book. You can tell I already have a busy year ahead, but if I can find the time, I'm sure my adoring fans would welcome a continuation of my story. Learn French, travel to France, train a little brother or sister, write another book? It looks to be another big year for the Royal Pooch!

About the Authors

Born in New York City and transplanted to the South in high school, Kathy Manos Penn lives with her husband and their four-legged kids in Dunwoody, Georgia. She taught high school English before embarking on a three-decade career in banking, where, it seemed, she always ended up writing. While still working in the corporate world, she began a side job as a columnist for the local newspaper. She is now happily retired from banking but has no plans to retire from the joyful job of writing. Her first book, *The Ink Penn: Celebrating the Magic in the Everyday*, is a collection of her newspaper columns and is available on Amazon.

Lord Banjo was born in New Orleans and moved to Atlanta at a young age. He was inspired to tell his story when his mum showed him his doggie DNA results. *Lord Banjo the Royal Pooch* is his first book.

Keep up with the Royal Mum and Lord Banjo by visiting their website at kathymanospenn.com. Nothing would please the Royal Pooch more than if you were to submit an online review.